A Butterfly Story

Kimberly Clay

Art by Maureen Grace

On a hot summer night
with my mom and my dad
I went on a quest –
an adventure to have.

We came to a field
with flowers and plants
and beetles and birds
and spiders and ants

We stopped at a plant
that was tall and bright green.
My mom said
"Look here! Do you see what I see?"

I didn't at first —

I just saw a green leaf.
But then, there it was!
I could hardly believe . . .

The tiniest caterpillar
was just hanging out
on that leaf on a plant
in the field just now.

I wanted to grab it but dad said
"Don't touch!"
"We don't want to hurt it
or move it that much."

We watched it chow down
on its soft yummy leaf.
It ate and it ate
its favorite plant—
milkweed.

We snipped off the leaf
and carefully took
the caterpillar with us
and continued to look.

We found some more critters
then mom said,

"Now this!"

She showed a white speck that was easy to miss.

A monarch egg,
so tiny and white

on the back of a leaf,
hidden from sight.

We collected that leaf
and soon headed home
to keep our "cats" and our eggs
until they are grown.

The caterpillars went in a
nice screened-in house
with milkweed galore
to eat and hang out.

The eggs went away in a
small sealed box.
We'd have to wait for
those babies to POP!

As time went on

the caterpillars ate,
and **grew** and **grew** and

ate and ate.

Their house got messy,

"What is all that stuff?"

"It's **POOP!**" Dad said.

"We better clean up."

We kept feeding them milkweed
and cleaning their poop.
Then one day they did something,
our cute little group.

They got really big
and their eating slowed,
then they climbed to the top
of their little abode.

They hung upside down —
I thought something was wrong
but mom said,
"Don't touch!"
"They're where they belong."

They hung for awhile,
then to my surprise
one of them wiggled and
before my eyes . . .

it turned into a **chrysalis**
bright and green!
It was the craziest thing
I had ever seen!

Each caterpillar did it —
     they ate and they grew,
and wiggled and made
     their own chrysalis too.

We waited and waited —
would it ever emerge?
After days and days it
was finally his turn.

The chrysalis turned clear,
I could see it inside —
a **butterfly** was forming!
It could no longer hide.

It broke open and came out –
a beautiful sight!
It was orange and black
and looked just right.

It hung there awhile and
opened its wings.
It stretched and it fluttered –
the prettiest thing.

We gave it some time
to practice its skills . . .
to learn how to feel
how a butterfly feels.

Then when it was ready,
we opened the door
to give it some space
and the world to explore.

It flew right out
and went straight to the sky.

And I said farewell
to my sweet butterfly.

About the Author

Kimberly lives in the Chicago area and is mother to three kids who LOVE to read. After spending many nights reading bedtime stories (just ONE more!?), she decided to join in the fun! She's spent many summers raising monarch butterflies with her kids and loves sharing this fun passion with others.

Maureen studied watercolor many years ago and more recently learned digital art techniques. Her daughter, Kim, asked her to create images to match the story she wrote and it turned into a family project. Maureen has illustrated several children's books in the last few years and loves reading with her three grandkids.

Visit our website for more story books, notebooks, journals, activity books and music manuscripts.

www.kimmoe.com